That Awful
Jackie Oliver!

The nerve of that Jackie Oliver!

Didn't he know that Abbey Mars was a very popular kid?

Didn't she get invited to all the birthday parties?

Didn't she win the Halloween prize for the best monster noises?

Didn't kids say things like "Hi, Abbey. How's it going, Abbey?" and "What'll we do today, Abbey?"

Didn't he know all that?

The nerve of that Jackie Oliver!

Books by Judith Hollands

Bowser the Beautiful
The Ketchup Sisters: The Rescue of the Red-Blooded Librarian
The Ketchup Sisters: The Deeds of the Desperate Campers
The Like Potion
The Nerve of Abbey Mars

Available from MINSTREL Books

THE NERVE OF ABBEY MARS

by JUDITH HOLLANDS

illustrated by
DEE DeROSA

A MINSTREL® BOOK

PUBLISHED BY POCKET BOOKS

New York   London   Toronto   Sydney   Tokyo

A MINSTREL PAPERBACK *ORIGINAL*

A Minstrel Book published by
POCKET BOOKS, a division of Simon & Schuster Inc.
1230 Avenue of the Americas, New York, NY 10020

ISBN: 0-671-70762-0

First Minstrel Books printing February 1988

10 9 8 7 6 5 4 3 2

A MINSTREL BOOK and colophon are registered trademarks
of Simon & Schuster Inc.

Printed in the U.S.A.

For Natalie, who was almost Abbey

THE NERVE OF
ABBEY MARS

CHAPTER ONE

Abbey Mars was much too young for boy-friends. But she could tell a yucky boy from a nice boy any day. Jackie Oliver was yucky—*very*. But Jake Yancy was nice.

Of course Abbey had a lot more important things to think about. After all, she was getting older and learning more about the world every day.

She wondered how a person got to own a zoo.

1

She wondered why anyone would want to invent yogurt.

She wondered about all the little dots on her teacher's map. Could one person ever visit them all?

And she wondered why she had to be such a rotten speller.

"It's not just the spelling, Abbey," Mrs. Wissel said as she shuffled through a pile of papers. Abbey noticed most of them had little snowflake or cardinal stickers on them. Abbey's had a big *4X* on the top. That meant four wrong.

"It's these capital letters," Mrs. Wissel said. She snuffled loudly and reached for a Kleenex. Mrs. Wissel's nose was bright red again.

Abbey stared at her paper and tried to look serious. Underneath, a little voice was dying to say, *But I like capital letters—they look so important.*

Mrs. Wissel wiped her nose and reached

for a red pen. She tapped at some words on Abbey's paper.

TurKee

CooKIe

POKit

LOk

"They pop up in the strangest places, Abbey. Like right in the middle or at the end of a word. Mrs. Wissel shook her head. "Don't use a capital letter unless you need to. You really must study these rules."

Abbey suddenly felt squirmy. She didn't want Mrs. Wissel to know that she hated to study.

Mrs. Wissel reached into her desk and pulled out a sheet of paper. Abbey had seen it before.

RULES FOR USING CAPITAL LETTERS

"Okay, Mrs. Wissel," Abbey said as she took the paper. She had three more just like it stuffed somewhere in her desk.

As Abbey shuffled toward her seat, Jackie Oliver grinned up at her. His desk was the first one in the first row.

Why, he's been listening! Abbey thought wildly. *I just know it.*

Roberta Bendix walked up and slapped Jackie's spelling paper down on his desk. Abbey saw a big *2X* on the top. No snowflake. No cardinal. Abbey grinned widely.

Jackie's face fell into a frown.

Just as Abbey thought she was safely past him, she heard a little whispery "Abba-abba-beep-BEEP-beep."

Abbey whirled around but Jackie was innocently writing his corrections. She wanted to bop him on top of his curly head. To make a big, awful-looking dent.

"Abbey!" Mrs. Wissel called. She was reaching for her little bottle of Nasa-Free. "Get back to your seat now and start on those corrections."

S-z-z—z-eet! S-zzzz-zeet! Mrs. Wissel squeezed the Nasa-Free into each side of her nose. Then S-s-s-ZUNK! s-s-S-ZUNK! She snuffled so loudly, Abbey gritted her teeth.

Mrs. Wissel was too busy with her allergies to care about Jackie Oliver and his spaceship noises.

Abbey bit her lip and marched all the way back to her seat. She swore she heard a couple more "beep-beeps" along the way.

The nerve of that Jackie Oliver!

Didn't he know Abbey Mars was a very popular kid?

Didn't she get invited to all the birthday parties?

Didn't she win the Halloween prize for the best monster noises? No kid dressed as Little Bo-Peep had ever done that before.

Didn't kids say things like "Hi, Abbey. How's it going, Abbey?" and "What'll we do today, Abbey?"

Didn't teachers pick her to read to the class because she wasn't afraid of crowds?

Didn't he know all that?

The nerve of that Jackie Oliver!

Abbey hadn't liked him for one minute ever since he'd come to Mrs. Wissel's class from Ohio. With his curled-up, lumpy-looking hair and his baggy, fish-colored eyes.

Nobody had ever picked on Abbey before. Nobody had ever said a word about her face or her floppy hair. Nobody had ever noticed her nose looked sort of like a kidney bean. Nobody had ever listened to the teacher talk about her capital letters. Nobody had ever done that!

Of course, Abbey had made it clear that she wouldn't put up with that sort of thing. She'd put on her wild gorilla look and raise

her fist. Then she'd snarl, "You want your face pushed in?"

That always stopped it until Jackie Oliver came along.

When Abbey raised her fist and snarled at Jackie, he'd just laughed. LAUGHED! Then he'd gone off with a bunch of boys and had come back later. He'd pointed at her and hollered:

Abbey Mars, Abbey Mars
Abba-abba-Abbey
With a face from outer space
Beep-beep-beep!

Then most of the boys had laughed. And some of the girls, too. Abbey had stood with her mouth opened up like a train tunnel.

Ever since then, there had been a lot of beeping in Mrs. Wissel's class.

Abbey settled into her seat and frowned. Just thinking about all of it made her want to do something really bad to Jackie Oliver. Like feed him to wild animals. Or tie him up in a big box and send him to the South Pole.

But Abbey was smart enough to know those things might not work. Wild animals might want more than one little kid to eat. What would she do then? And how would she carry such a big box to the post office?

"Abbey, are you doing those corrections?" Mrs. Wissel was standing at her desk looking out at her.

Abbey nodded and picked up her yellow pencil.

She shook her head as she looked again at the red x's.

It just didn't make sense.

If tree was t-r-e-e and Abbey was A-b-b-e-y, then how did you tell if turkey was turkee or turkey? Abbey had picked turkee, which was wrong, of course.

Then, just when a girl got used to worry-

9

ing about ee and ey, along came a word like cookie!

Abbey shook her head again as she wrote *cookie* five times. Whoever thought up spelling must have a hard time making up his mind.

She stared at the next red *x*. PokIT. What was wrong with that?

Abbey looked over at Suzy McNally. She was reading a book. Beside her lay her perfect little spelling paper with a snowflake on top. Suzy was always getting A+ or 100's.

Abbey leaned as far as she could and counted down seven. P-o-c-k-e-t! How silly! How was she supposed to think of putting a *c* before the *k?* And *ET!* Everybody knew that was somebody from outer space.

Outer space. A face from outer space. There it was again. Abbey shot a quick look at Jackie Oliver and his ugly, curly head.

Imagine anybody making up such a thing about her!

Kids picked on Justine Hamm, but that was because she cried about everything. And Darren Parker tripped a lot. But nobody—NOBODY—had ever said such an awful thing about Abbey. And for the first time in her life she felt sort of ashamed of her name.

She remembered how nice it had been to be a Perky Pee-Wee at Miss Allen's Nursery School. Miss Allen liked capital letters. Every day Abbey had written ABBEY MARS across the top of her paper. Miss Allen had smiled and said, "Excellent, Abbey."

And not one single person had beeped.

CHAPTER TWO

Tara Barnes was taking a long time at the drinking fountain. Abbey got tired of staring at the back of her blue jeans. She had little birds and pink hearts stitched all over the pockets. Abbey jabbed a finger into one of the bird's eyeballs.

Tara stood up straight and grabbed at her rear end.

"Hey!" Tara turned around. Her eyebrows looked all bunched up. "Quit poking!"

"Well, hurry up!" Abbey hissed. "A kid could die back here waiting for you."

Tara rolled her eyes all around and giggled. "You just don't want to miss Jake." She was pointing toward the front of the room and wiping water from her chin.

Abbey looked behind her.

Jake Yancy was standing at the front board, holding Mrs. Wissel's ruler.

His hair was kind of butter-colored and laid down nice and flat all over. His nose was curvy and cute. And he looked very clean.

Mrs. Wissel was asking him to point to the parts of a letter. The greeting, the body, the closing. Abbey could see that Jake Yancy was a nice boy. And smart, too.

Abbey gulped a few swallows of water and hurried to her desk.

"Thank you, Jake," Mrs. Wissel said. "You did an excellent job. Does anyone have any questions about letter-writing?"

As Jake passed by Abbey's desk, she gave him one of her smartest-looking smiles.

"All right, everyone," Mrs. Wissel said. She dropped her chalk onto the chalk tray. A little cloud of chalk dust puffed up into the air.

Oh, no! thought Abbey. *When will she learn not to drop the chalk?*

"A-a-A-A-CHOO!" Mrs. Wissel wasn't ready with her Kleenex. She sneezed right onto her finger.

It must be awful to walk around sneezing all the time, Abbey thought. But, if Abbey were allergic, she'd try her best to sit behind Jackie. Then she could sneeze all over the back of his head.

Mrs. Wissel was waving at the calendar on the front bulletin board. Today was February 1, and she'd taken down the snowman picture. Above the word *February*, she'd tacked a new picture. Two fat hearts were holding hands and winking at each other.

"This is an excellent month for us to work on letter-writing," Mrs. Wissel said. "We'll all be sending valentines later this month. I thought it was time we had our own mailbox."

She reached into a big bag and brought out a little blue-and-red-paper mailbox. It looked just like a real one—only smaller.

Abbey leaned forward. Now this was interesting. Abbey loved mail, but she never got too much. Just a few cards on her birthday and at Christmastime. Her mother had once said that Abbey could have some of her bills. But she'd just been kidding.

"I have another surprise for you, too," Mrs. Wissel said. She lifted some cardboard boxes up onto the shelf by the window. Each box had lots of other little boxes inside it.

"This will be our post office," she said.

"I want everyone to write their names on these labels."

Mrs. Wissel began to pass out some little white rectangles. "Then each of you can have your own box.

"Try to write two letters this morning—one to a girl and one to a boy. And do more if you have time. That way everybody should get at least one letter."

Abbey couldn't wait to begin her letters. First she wrote to Tara Barnes.

Dear TaRA,
    Can You Com oVeR tooDAY?

MY Mom sAys ITs' o.K. to pLAY
                        CirKus.

BUT We KaN'T UsE RoLLo foR
                        a PonY.

He's ONLEE a DoG.
                    LoVE,
                        ABBEY

There. Abbey folded up the letter three times. Then she wrote "TaRA" on it and walked up to the blue-and-red mailbox. When she passed the post office, she saw her name under one of the spaces. Near the bottom she saw "Jake Y.," printed neatly on a label.

Abbey wondered. Did she dare write a letter to Jake Yancy? What would she say? "You're nice?" NO. That was awful. Kids her age didn't say things like that. They just thought about them.

Abbey ended up writing to Bobby Madden.

WeN will You BrinG in Yor
ParRoT?
I Hav SoM KrakErS foR
                    HiM.

            LOVE,
            ABBEY

Abbey could hardly wait until Mrs. Wissel was done with reading groups. It was getting closer and closer to lunchtime. But Mrs. Wissel was still busy with The Sky Riders and their workbooks. When would she pass out the letters?

"Uh-A-A-CHOO!" Mrs. Wissel stood up at last and turned toward the front of the room. "Oh, dear," she said. "It's time to eat and I haven't even delivered your letters. You'll have to wait until after lunch."

Everybody moaned. Mrs. Wissel put her hands on her hips. She looked tired today.

"Well, okay," she said. "Suzy, I'll bet you could do a good job as our postman—I mean, lady. Why don't you go ahead and deliver the mail? Then you can meet us at the lunchroom."

Abbey wished she could be the post-lady. It was just like Suzy to get all the good jobs.

When lunch was over, everybody hurried back to the room. Letters! Abbey had five. Nora Letterman had six. Justine Hamm had only one.

The first one was from Tara. She wanted Abbey to go to the movies with her!

The second one was from Kevin Malley. He wanted to know if Abbey liked green Jell-O.

She unfolded the third letter and stopped suddenly. It wasn't a letter! It was a drawing! A stupid, horrible drawing of a spaceship with steps coming out of it.

Underneath, it said:

Abbey's house.

Beep-beep-beep.

Nobody's name was on it, but Abbey knew who had sent it, all right.

Abbey's face felt hot all over. She grabbed the picture and rushed up to Mrs. Wissel's desk. Oh, boy, would she tell on that Jackie Oliver!

But somebody was already at the teacher's desk. Mrs. Wissel was hugging Justine Hamm! Justine was crying and sniffing and hiccoughing. Abbey could see her shoulders jerking and shaking. Justine's nose sounded almost as stuffed up as Mrs. Wissel's.

Abbey stood quietly at the desk. It didn't seem right to try to get Mrs. Wissel's attention. Justine looked pretty worked up.

"They didn't even"—snuffle-hic—"sign it!" she said, sobbing.

Abbey looked down at Mrs. Wissel's desk. There, done in purple crayon, was a fat pig lying on a platter.

Underneath, it said:

Justine Hamm, Justine Hamm
Piggy-piggy-piggy
Lying in a pan
Oink-oink-oink

Abbey just stared. Whoever had done that drawing had done the spaceship, too! Somebody who had a purple crayon! Somebody who liked to make up mean little songs!

"Jackie Oliver did that!" Abbey yelled out loud.

Justine stopped crying.

Mrs. Wissel turned toward Abbey. "Why, how can you know that, Abbey?" Mrs. Wissel asked.

"It's not true!" Jackie Oliver shouted. "I wrote to Lisa and Jake. You saw me, Kevin." Jackie poked Kevin Malley with the eraser end of his pencil.

Mrs. Wissel stood up. "Lisa, Jake," she said. "Did you receive letters from Jackie? Please bring them to me."

Lisa and Jake both came to the front of the room carrying pieces of paper. Abbey peered over Mrs. Wissel's shoulder. The letters were written in pencil—not crayon.

Mrs. Wissel studied them carefully. Then she made everyone sit down.

"All right, class," she said. Now she looked angry *and* tired. "Someone sent unkind letters to Justine and Abbey. It's hard to believe one of my students could do something like that. I don't know for sure who made these drawings, but I'll have *no more* of it. Is that clear?"

Abbey stared at the floor. Mrs. Wissel sounded very upset. That Jackie! Mrs. Wissel glanced at the clock and then walked over to her locker. She was putting on her coat! Mrs. Wissel was leaving! Abbey had never seen a teacher give up before.

There was a loud knock at the door and a lady with a smiling face poked her head in. "Are you ready for me, Mrs. Wissel?" she asked.

Mrs. Wissel dabbed at her red nose with a Kleenex. "I'm going to go home for the rest of today, class," she said. "I need some rest. But I won't forget about this." Mrs. Wissel's eyes moved all over the room. Then she pulled up the collar of her coat and left.

CHAPTER THREE

Justine kept breaking into little sobs all afternoon. At last the substitute teacher sent her to the nurse.

The substitute's name was Mrs. Carvers. She had very pink cheeks and great big teeth that showed because she smiled a lot.

Mrs. Wissel had left so fast that Mrs. Carvers had mixed up the plans. "We'll just do a spelling lesson," Mrs. Carvers said as she reached for the book. "Everybody likes spelling, now, don't they?"

Abbey decided she didn't like Mrs. Carvers very much. She called the kids "children." Before they went outside, she even helped some girls put on their coats.

"How about a nice little game of Ring-Around-the-Rosy?" Mrs. Carvers asked as she clapped her mittens together. Her breath was puffing out of her smiling mouth.

Abbey couldn't believe it. Most of the kids walked away from Mrs. Carvers pretty fast. Abbey wouldn't be caught *dead* playing Ring-Around-the-Rosy. Didn't Mrs. Carvers know that was a baby game? What did she look like, anyway—some kind of Perky Pee-Wee?

"Did you see Justine?" Tara asked as she and Abbey climbed to the top of the jungle bars.

Abbey twirled her head around and searched the playground. Justine was sitting on the steps. She had her hands dug down into her coat pockets.

"Her eyes are all puffed up," Tara said. She was squeezing her eyelids shut, pretending she was Justine. "I've never seen anybody so upset about one little note," Tara said. "I wonder what it said."

Tara looked at Abbey. Abbey wanted to tell about the piggy in the pan. But something stopped her.

Jackie Oliver had sent two terrible notes—not just one. What if everybody knew about the piggy *and* about the spaceship?

"Let's chase Kevin!" Abbey cried suddenly. "He's got on his string-bean hat!"

She and Tara hopped to the ground. Then, screaming at the top of their lungs, they raced after Kevin Malley and his funny green hat.

Mrs. Carvers ended up scolding both of

them for acting like wild little Indians. Abbey decided Mrs. Carvers liked quiet, perfect little girls like Suzy McNally. But Abbey didn't care.

She lay in the snow and made shapes and letters. She'd been thinking about it all afternoon.

Jackie Oliver was more than just a yucky boy. He was mean. He *wanted* Abbey to feel absolutely rotten about her name. And Jackie had lied to Mrs. Wissel.

Right then and there, Abbey decided she was going to fix Jackie Oliver. Somehow, some way. It had to be done.

CHAPTER FOUR

Mr. Mars was quizzing Abbey on her spelling words. He always looked as if he were trying to have a good time.

"Okay, let's look at this next one," Mr. Mars said in a peppy voice. "Well . . . *cookie* . . . that's not so hard, is it?"

He picked up a chocolate graham cracker from a plate on the table. "Hmm," he said. "Let's concentrate." Then he winked at Abbey and his face got serious.

"Okay, Abbey," he said, "think about the sounds you hear. Cook-ie . . . cook-ie."

Mr. Mars broke the word into two little parts. Abbey could tell he thought this made things easier for her.

Abbey sort of enjoyed watching her father do spelling. Ever since she got a U in spelling, he'd been working with her three nights a week.

"Don't you want to read the paper?" Abbey asked. She could see her father's favorite chair waiting for him in the living room.

"Of course," Mr. Mars said. "But I can do that later. We've got more important things to do."

Abbey could see how much her father wanted to help. But it was seven o'clock. By the time her father got through the list, it would be time for her shower. Then she'd have to go to bed.

Abbey slid off the chair. She tried to look businesslike.

"I think I need to do some serious studying tonight, Dad," she said. "Mrs. Wissel wants us to be independent thinkers. Would you mind if I finished these up by myself?"

Mr. Mars looked startled. "Well, I don't see why not . . ." he began. His eyes followed Abbey as she headed for the stairs. He still had the graham cracker in his hand.

"Thanks," Abbey called as she made her escape. It was time to put her plans into action.

A little while later Abbey's mother came up to her room. She had a worried look on her face. "What *are* you doing up here, honey?" she asked.

Abbey was reading Chapter Five in her

spelling book—the one about making words rhyme. She had all her pillows piled into a nice cozy bunch. Then she'd stuffed herself in the middle. Sort of like a sandwich.

"Oh . . ." Mrs. Mars seemed surprised. "Why, you're still working. I didn't think . . . well . . . you don't usually . . . oh, never mind." She walked softly out and closed the door behind her.

"Back, track, snack," Abbey read out loud. "Words that rhyme have the same middle and ending sounds. Only the beginning sounds are different."

It didn't seem very hard. If mean old Jackie Oliver could do it, so could Abbey Mars.

"Snake, break . . . uh *. . . cake."* Abbey made those up by herself. She planned to write some little letters of her own to Jackie Oliver. But she'd have to be careful

about her spelling. She didn't want to take any chances.

She rolled over onto her back. "If I'm going to write letters," she said, "I'm going to make *sure* he can read them."

CHAPTER FIVE

By Tuesday, Abbey had a whole lot of letters ready. She'd decided to mail one a day until she ran out. Then she'd make more.

Mrs. Wissel was hanging cupids from the overhead lights. She wasn't even looking.

Abbey unfolded her first letter. She read it over carefully. It was perfect.

YOUR HAIR LOOKS LIKE O's
YOU'VE GOT FATSO TOES
YOU'rE SO DIRTY YOU ITCH,
SO STICK YOUR HEAD IN
                    A DITCH.

            LOVE, ABBEY

Abbey smiled. Even if Mrs. Wissel
found out, how could she be angry? After
all, Abbey had been nice enough to sign
her name. Neatly, too.

Abbey worried a little. Did that make
sense? But then she decided it was worth it
. . . just to see Jackie's face.

She skipped all the way to the mailbox.
She hummed as she finished her heart

mobile. She answered all the questions in her Stepping Stones reading group.

"Why are you smiling at your tuna sandwich?" Tara asked in the lunchroom.

Abbey kept on chewing and smiling. But she didn't tell about the letters.

Each day the letters got better.

Your eyes are Yuck.

Your hAIr is Yick

DoctoR, DoctoR,

You Look so Sick.

You'd BeTTER CALL The NEaREST NuRSE,

BECAuSE You BeLoNG
in A Big BLACk HEArse!

LoVe, ABBEY

Abbey began looking up words in the big dictionary in the library. When she needed help, Mrs. Felton, the librarian, would come over.

Abbey had to check on the spelling of *totally* and *disgusting*. And she needed a word to rhyme with *slimy*.

"Abbey, I'm glad to see you are showing so much interest in the library," Mrs. Felton said. "I think I'll just tell your teacher how pleased I am."

Good, thought Abbey. Then if she did get caught, Mrs. Felton could come and say nice things about her.

But Abbey wasn't worrying so much lately about getting caught. She spent almost every minute watching Jackie's face. She never did seem to look up at the right time. She never did see him open a letter.

"Get your fat eyes off of me!" Jackie hissed as he walked to the pencil sharpener.

"Can't take it, can you?" Abbey answered. She put on a pleased-looking smile.

"Beep-beep," Jackie said as he walked back past her.

Abbey felt as if things were popping inside her. The nerve of that Jackie Oliver! The next letter was even better.

Nobody likes you.
Everybody hates you
Your guts are pea-green
You're the ugliest we've seen
If you would go away,
It would be a happy day!

Love, Abbey

CHAPTER SIX

Tara was stuffing her coat into her locker. "Did you bring your valentines?" she asked as she lifted a paper bag and shook it at Abbey. She was wearing heart-shaped barrettes in her hair.

"Uh-huh," Abbey said as she bent over and tugged at the wrinkles in her red tights. Somehow, her red tights always got baggy in the knees. She stood up and tucked her own grocery bag full of valentines under her arm.

Finally it was time for the Valentine's Day party. Abbey was excited. She had her valentines all signed and ready to mail. She'd saved the best one for Jake. It was a little gray kitten. At the top it said:

VALENTINE, YOU'RE P-U-R-R-R-F-ECT.

All in capital letters.

Then she had an extra-special letter just for Jackie. She'd spent a lot of time writing it and checking the spelling:

HAPPy Un-VaLENTINE to You

You BeLoNg IN A Zoo

You Look LiKe A RHinoceRoS

AND You SMeLL LiKe ONe too!

LoVE, ABBEY

45

Abbey wasn't sure if a rhinoceros smelled bad or not. But she figured that if they hung around in the mud all day, they probably did.

She wanted to draw a big dirty-looking rhinoceros, but she wasn't so good at art.

All the kids were talking like crazy when in walked Mrs. Carvers!

"Where is Mrs. Wissel?" somebody yelled.

"She's having a bad day," Mrs. Carvers said as she tapped one side of her nose. "So I thought I'd come and help out. Oh, I do love parties!" She was clapping and smiling again.

Abbey felt sort of droopy. No Mrs. Wissel? After all her decorating and letter-writing lessons? The room looked so pretty with all the glittery mobiles and dangling cupids. It just didn't seem right without Mrs. Wissel.

But a party *was* still a party, after all.

Parents would still bring in punch and cookies. The kids would play games and read their valentines. And Jackie Oliver would feel absolutely rotten—she hoped.

To get in the spirit, Abbey cut out some red paper hearts and pasted them onto her skirt. School paste only lasted a little while. By the time she got home, she could have it all picked off. Her mother would never know.

Abbey made her skirt twirl as she got up to pass in her math paper.

At one o'clock, Mrs. Carvers clapped her hands. "Don't forget to mail your valentines," she said. "Then we'll play a little game while we're watching for our visitors."

Oh, no! thought Abbey. *Ring-Around-the-Rosy?* Abbey was close. Mrs. Carvers wanted to play The Farmer in the Dell.

Some Valentine's Day game, Abbey thought. Last year Mr. Hunter had had a

Heart Hunt. He'd stapled little paper hearts and stuffed them with candy. Then he'd hidden them all over the room. Even last year seemed more grown up than this year!

Mrs. Carvers was tapping her foot and singing loudly. "Come on, everyone!" she yelled when nobody sang with her.

It had been a long time since Abbey had played The Farmer in the Dell. And it was a holiday, after all. Pretty soon she was singing along at the top of her lungs.

"Oh, the wife takes a dog, the wife takes a dog . . ."

Tara grabbed at Abbey's arm. Around and around the room they swung, acting pretty crazy. Abbey twirled front and back, front and back. She felt like part of a human roller coaster.

Mrs. Carvers was yelling "Settle down now!" from somewhere far away.

All the kids were singing the next line.

"Oh, the dog takes a cat, the dog takes a cat . . ."

Abbey saw Jake Yancy's face whirl in front of her. *Why not?* she thought, and she reached out and pulled on Jake's shoulder.

Then a terrible thing happened. Jake jumped away from Abbey as if she were trying to murder him.

"Don't touch me!" he hollered. "You stay away!"

Everybody stopped dancing and singing and stared.

Jake's eyes had a funny, crazy look in them.

He pointed at Abbey. "You've got a lot of nerve, Abbey Mars! A lot of nerve!"

Jake almost looked as if he were getting ready to cry. Mrs. Carvers rushed over. She sank to her knees and sort of threw herself around him.

Jake twisted and shook her arms away.

"Leave me alone!" he yelled. "I know what you think!" He waved a hand at all the kids. "What you all think. And you're all just . . . a bunch of . . ." Now Jake *was* crying! "A bunch of . . . *big dummies!*" he blubbered.

He raced out of the room and Mrs. Carvers sent Bobby Madden running after him.

All the kids sat quietly at their desks and ate their cookies when the room mothers came. Mrs. Carvers stood out in the hallway talking to Jake.

Abbey couldn't understand it. Maybe Jake really hated The Farmer in the Dell.

"Abbey." It was Mrs. Carvers. "May I see you in the hallway, please?"

When Abbey stepped outside the door, Jake looked at her and sort of shivered all over.

"She's the one," he said, pointing at her nose. "She wrote them all."

Mrs. Carvers was holding a stack of letters.

"Abbey, did you send these to poor little Jake?" She pushed the letters into Abbey's hands.

Abbey slowly opened one paper after another.

They were all her letters to Jackie Oliver! How did Jake get them?

"But I don't get it," Abbey said. "I put these in the mailbox. Suzy was supposed to put them in Jackie Oliver's box."

"Suzy!" Mrs. Carvers called as she opened the door to the classroom. "Could you step out here for a little minute?"

Suzy joined the group in the hall. She looked first at Jake, then at Abbey, and then at the pile of letters. She seemed really nervous. Suzy never got called into the hall when there was trouble.

"I sent all these to Jackie Oliver," Abbey said to Suzy. "And you gave them to Jake."

Suzy looked at Abbey. Then she grabbed the top letter and turned it over and over. "But that's not what you wrote," she said. She was pointing to some printing on the outside.

What was she talking about?

"Right here," Suzy said. "Here's the name right here."

Abbey snatched back the paper and looked at it. Printed in her own handwriting were these letters:

$$Jake Y$$

"See?" Suzy said. "It says 'Jake Y.' Jake Y.—that's him." She waved a finger at Jake. "Jake Yancy."

Abbey wanted to die. It *did* say "JaKeY," but that wasn't what she'd meant! She'd meant to write *Jackie!* But, oh, why did she have to be such a rotten speller? A rotten speller who loved capital letters!

All this time Jake had been getting those awful notes. And Jackie—mean old Jackie—hadn't even seen one!

Abbey wished she could find some wild animals. Some hungry, wild animals. So hungry they'd eat any little kid—even if she was stupid in spelling.

CHAPTER SEVEN

The next day Mrs. Wissel was back.

"Oh, Mrs. Wissel, may I see you out here, please?" Mr. Denton, the principal, was leaning in Mrs. Wissel's doorway and waving a finger at her.

Mrs. Wissel came to the door. She didn't look so tired and her nose was just a little pink. Abbey wanted to smile and throw her arms around her. But this was no time for that.

"This young lady has asked for a transfer," Mr. Denton said.

"A . . . what?" Mrs. Wissel looked shocked.

"She says she must be switched to another classroom."

"For the good of the class," Abbey said clearly. She didn't want any more trouble. She hated to say good-bye to all her friends. But some things had to be done.

Mrs. Wissel leaned down to look closely at Abbey. "Is this about what happened at the party?" she asked.

Abbey nodded.

"I think I can handle this, Mr. Denton," Mrs. Wissel said.

Mr. Denton looked first at Abbey and then at Mrs. Wissel. "I hope so," he said.

Mrs. Wissel waited until he was gone before she spoke again. She bent down on

her knees and looked right into Abbey's eyes.

"You know, Abbey," she began, "what you did might not have been a very good idea. But you didn't really mean any harm. I know Jake understands. I've already talked with him."

"You have?" Abbey asked hopefully.

Mrs. Wissel nodded. "The important thing, even when things really get you down, is *not to give up*. She tapped her pink nose and sniffed a little. "Do you know what I mean?"

Abbey laughed. Mrs. Wissel wasn't angry!

"I don't think Jackie will be writing any more letters either," she added.

Abbey was surprised to hear this.

Mrs. Wissel took a purple crayon out of her skirt pocket. "I found this and a rotten banana peel stuffed in an old lunchbag. I found it when I cleaned out the closet the day before the party. Jackie's name was on the bag."

"Did he tell the truth?" Abbey asked.

Mrs. Wissel smiled. "Oh, I finally got it out of him. I have my ways."

Abbey beamed! Mrs. Wissel wasn't angry. Jackie had been caught. And maybe . . . maybe Jake could forgive her.

Abbey walked slowly into the classroom. She felt like a new girl on the first day of school. She hurried up her row to her desk. But nobody said a word. And no beeps, either.

Tara was leaning sideways in her seat. "Pssst! Abbey," she said. She held out her hand and Abbey saw a little white note. More letters? For a minute she almost shook her head.

"It's from Justine," Tara whispered.

Abbey grapped up the note and opened it.

It read:

Abbey,
    I heard what you did.

Want to be friends?

                    Justine

A little yellow heart candy was also wrapped up in the note. Abbey turned it over. It said:

HOT 'STUFF

Abbey straightened up in her chair. She smiled over at Justine. Justine giggled. Abbey had never seen her look so perky.

Things were working out after all.

CHAPTER EIGHT

"Now, everyone, let's get back to our spelling quiz," Mrs. Wissel said brightly. "We'll begin with the words from chapters Fifteen through Twenty-five. Anyone who misses must sit and write his word twenty times."

Abbey felt a little droopy again. Mrs. Wissel was a terrific teacher. But why did she have such a big thing about spelling?

Mrs. Wissel started with the last person in the last row. Anyone who got his or her word right could stand up. If they missed, they had to sit down and write their corrections.

Around and around the room they went, over and over again. Abbey spelled *itch, track, ditch, ugly,* and *nurse*—all correctly.

Finally it was just Suzy, Jake, and Abbey standing up. Abbey was amazed. She had always been one of the first ones who missed her word.

"*Noise,*" Mrs. Wissel said, and Jake frowned. Abbey was glad Mrs. Wissel hadn't called on her.

"N-o-y-s-e?" Jake didn't sound too sure of himself.

"Sorry. N-o-i-s-e, Jake," Mrs. Wissel said. "But that was a good try.

"Well, well." Mrs. Wissel looked at Abbey and Suzy. "I've run out of words. I guess I'll have to think of something harder. Let's see . . . how about. . . ?" She seemed to spot something on her desk. "How about . . . *dictionary?*"

Suzy looked as if she were thinking hard. Her forehead had little mashed-up lines in it. "D-i-c-. . ." Suzy frowned harder. "Uh . . . s-h-u-n-a-r-e?"

"Sorry, Suzy," Mrs. Wissel said. "That's not it. . . . Abbey?" Mrs. Wissel looked so hopeful. Abbey really wanted to get it right.

Abbey closed her eyes and tried to re-member the letters on Mrs. Felton's book. "D-i-c-t-i-o-n-a-r-. . ." Abbey stopped. Oh, no. How was she going to spell that sound at the end. EE? EY? IE? "E-e?" Abbey said, making a little question.

"Oh-h-h-h, I'm sorry, Abbey," Mrs. Wissel said. "Not quite right. But I'm proud of you both for trying. Especially

Won't you be
my Valentine?

you, Abbey. I don't think you've ever made it this far."

Abbey hopped back up out of her seat. "How about *rhinoceros?*" she cried. "I can spell that!"

Mrs. Wissel looked as if she wanted to laugh. "No, that's all right, Abbey. I can tell how hard you've been studying."

Studying? Abbey thought. "Was that what she'd been doing? All those nights in her room. With her spelling book. And at the library. She, Abbey Mars, *had been studying?* Well . . . what do you know— maybe she had!

"How about a round of applause for our two best spellers today?" Mrs. Wissel asked.

Abbey stood next to Suzy as everybody clapped.

Before she went home, Abbey drew a picture of Mrs. Wissel and put it on her desk. She made the nose bright pink.

It said:

KEEP SMILING

DON'T GIVE UP!

CHAPTER NINE

When Abbey's father heard about the spelling quiz, he looked really proud. "I'd say that deserves a trip to the mall," he said. "And five dollars to spend."

Abbey had never felt so important. Five dollars!

She bought a poster of two monkeys scratching each other's back. And a big slice of pizza. And a book of crossword puzzles for ages six through ten. Crossword puzzles were for good spellers.

As they were getting ready to leave, she saw Jake Yancy standing with his big brother. Jake was eating some kind of pink ice cream.

"Hey, Abbey!" he yelled. "How's it going?"

"One of your friends?" Mr. Mars asked.

"Well . . . sort of," Abbey said shyly. Mr. Mars started walking over toward Jake and his brother. Abbey's insides felt as if they were running away without her.

"Boy, those were some letters you wrote to Jackie," Jake said. "I'm sure glad you didn't mean them for me."

Abbey looked up. "You really think so?" she asked, studying Jake's face. He looked like good old, smart, clean Jake again.

"For sure. You've got a lot of nerve, Abbey Mars, saying all those things." Jake giggled and wiped some pink stuff off his mouth.

"Here, you want some?" He stuck his cone up to her face.

Abbey politely took a lick. It made a funny tingle in her mouth. "Mmm. That's pretty good. What is it, anyway?" she asked.

"Frozen yogurt," Jake said. "Strawberry. It's my favorite."

Yogurt! Abbey watched Jake take a big, greedy lick.

What a terrific invention! thought Abbey Mars as she and her father headed home.

About the Author and Illustrator

JUDITH WINSHIP HOLLANDS was graduated from Boston University and has taught elementary school as well as gifted education. She has published both fiction and nonfiction for children and thinks that a children's author "must, above all, draw on his or her memory." Her constant companions are her two dogs, Bowser and Biff, and her two cats, Rockwell and Buttermilk. She believes "a little bit of Abbey Mars is in every elementary-school student." Her Minstrel Book titles also include *Bowser the Beautiful; The Ketchup Sisters: The Rescue of the Red-Blooded Librarian; The Ketchup Sisters: The Deeds of the Desperate Campers;* and *The Like Potion.*

DEE DEROSA grew up in Colorado, graduated from Syracuse University, and now lives in a rural area of New York State. She is married and has two children, three horses, and one dog. Mrs. DeRosa is also the illustrator of *Bowser the Beautiful; The Ketchup Sisters: The Rescue of the Red-Blooded Librarian;* and *The Ketchup Sisters: The Deeds of the Desperate Campers,* by Judith Hollands.

POCKET BOOKS PRESENTS

MINSTREL BOOKS™

THE FUN BOOKS YOU WILL NOT WANT TO MISS!!